TWO MORE PINTS

RODDY DOYLE

Two More Pints

JONATHAN CAPE
LONDON

Published by Jonathan Cape 2014

2 4 6 8 10 9 7 5 3 1

First published in Great Britain in 2014 by
Jonathan Cape
20 Vauxhall Bridge Road,
London SW1V 2SA

www.vintage-books.co.uk
A Penguin Random House Company

Penguin
Random House
UK

global.penguinrandomhouse.com

A CIP catalogue record for this book
is available from the British Library

ISBN 9780224101899

Typeset in Plantin by Palimpsest Book Production Limited,
Falkirk, Stirlingshire

Printed and bound in Great Britain by Clays Ltd, St Ives plc

To my father, Rory Doyle
8th December 1923 – March 16th 2014

TWO MORE PINTS

— Wha' d'yeh make of the photographs?
 — Wha' photographs?
 — Kate Middleton.
 — Who's she?
 — You're jokin'.
 — I'm not.
 — You have to be.
 — I'm not. I lose track o' them all.
 — She's look it, she's married to Prince William.
 — Which one's he?
 — For fuck sake—
 — I know who yeh mean. Topless pictures.
 — Exactly.
 — An' riots in all the Arab places because o' them.
 — No, listen—
 — Egypt an' Australia an' tha'.
 — No – that's a fillum abou' Muhammad.
 — Topless?
 — No – that's the French cartoons.
 — Wha'?
 — Let's just concentrate on the Middleton pictures.
 — Your man, Muhammad – he's dead, isn't he?
 — You're gettin' distracted. Listen.
 — Wha'?
 — You're out on your balcony.
 — I don't have a balcony.
 — You're out the back. An' it's a lovely day.
 — Okay.
 — You take your top off—
 — So I'm topless.
 — You are.
 — An' me tits are bigger than your woman's.

— They are.

— Serious – they are.

— So are mine.

— Desperate, isn't it?

— We'll get back to tha'. Annyway. You don't know it, but someone's takin' photos of yeh.

— The cunt. Who?

— A paparazzi. Me, say. An' I sell the pictures to the *Star*.

— Okay.

— For a fortune.

— Fair enough.

— I brought me camera.

— Give us a hand with this zip.

3-10-12

— *Top o' the Pops.*

— Wha'?

— D'you remember watchin' *Top o' the Pops* when you were a kid?

— Yeah – 'course.

— Pan's People.

— Fuckin' hell. The first women.

— Wha'?

— For me, like. That was wha' it felt like. I remember them dancin' durin' a Status Quo song.

— 'Down Down'.

— You remember it as well.

— I do, yeah.

— They were un-fuckin'-believable.

— They fuckin' were.

— An' I remember thinkin' – it sounds fuckin' ridiculous – but I remember thinkin', They're women!

— A eureka moment.

— Something like tha', yeah.

— An' it made you very happy.

— It fuckin' did.

— An' it still does.

— A bit, yeah.

— An' Jimmy Savile. When yeh saw him on *Top o' the Pops*. Wha' did yeh think?

— Fuckin' eejit.

— Yeah – me too. A gobshite. But never annythin' else.

— No.

— Yeh never thought you were lookin' at a fuckin' paedophile.

— Well, look it, I went to the Christian Brothers. I didn't

have to look at *Top o' the Pops* to know what a paedophile looked like.

— It's horrible but, isn't it?

— Fuckin' horrible.

— Makes yeh wonder how many more television celebs an' tha' were paedophiles back then.

— Nearly all o' them, I'd say.

— The lot.

— Except Morecambe an' Wise.

— They were sound.

— See Enda Kenny's on the cover of *Time*.

— Give me a shout when he's on the cover of *Playboy*.

— It's a big deal, but. He's the first Irishman to make the cover since, well – probably Obama.

— He's not Irish.

— Obama?

— Kenny – he's not fuckin' Irish.

— Wha'?

— He's from Mayo, yeah?

— Think so – somewhere over there.

— Then he's Moroccan.

— Wha'?

— I seen it on a thing – on the telly. The Moroccans came up from wherever the Moroccans come from—

— Morocco.

— Yeah. An' they settled in Mayo an' Galway an' tha'. Took it over, basically. An' the locals never noticed.

— Says nothin' abou' Morocco on the cover. The Celtic Comeback, it says.

— Me hole.

— Annyway, listen. They interviewed him—

— Did they interview Reilly as well, did they? Doctor fuckin' James.

— I don't think so—

— The Celtic Cunt. He'd try to sell them a second-hand ol' folks' home.

— Annyway—

— An' relocate New York to fuckin' Swords.

— Just fuckin' listen. Kenny wants to bring us back to the late '90s.

— Wha'?

— So he says.

— What's he on?

— Somethin' Moroccan, I'd say. But I'll tell yeh, if we are goin' back to the '90s, it's just as well yeh held on to tha' shirt.

— Fuck off.

17-10-12

— D'yeh read much?

   — Wha'? Books an' tha'?

— Yeah.

   — A bit. History – I like. The Nazis an' tha'. Why?

— I wouldn't mind readin' your man Mitt Romney's new one.

   — He has a book?

   — *Binders Full o' Women.*

— Great fuckin' title.

   — It's kind of a man's version o' *Fifty Shades o' Grey.* Far as I can make ou'.

   What's it abou'?

— The Governor of Massachew—. The one the Bee Gees used to sing about. Annyway, the women—

   — The binders o' them.

— Yeah – exactly. They're attracted to him and they want to ride the arse off him.

   — Grand.

— Cos he's a bollix.

   — Sounds realistic. A bit strange, but, isn't it? A presidential candidate havin' a book like that ou' a few weeks before the election.

   — He's after the men's book club vote, I'd say.

   — Could be his downfall, but.

   — How?

— The word – binders. Remember our own presidential fella who mentioned the brown envelope in the debate an' tha' was the end of him?

   — Yeah.

— Well, binders might be Mitt's brown envelope.

   — He's fucked.

— An' not like the fella in his book.

— *Brown Envelopes Full o' Women*. Would yeh buy tha' one?

— Jesus, m'n, you're makin' me weak.

— Which way are yeh votin'?

— I can't vote, bud.

— How come?

— I'm not American.

— Not tha' one. Our own one – the referendum, like.

— Another one? It's not fuckin' Europe again, is it?

— No—

— Fuckin' Hitler had the right idea there—

— Relax, for fuck sake. Take a fuckin' chill pill. This one is abou' protectin' children's rights.

— What's the point o' tha'? Jimmy's Savile's dead.

— It's not about Jimmy Savile.

— I know. There's Gary Glitter ou' there as well, an' the rest of them.

— No, listen—

— No, you listen. They – children, like – they already have their Xboxes an' their – fuckin' – tha' place where the young fellas nearly show off their tackle.

— Abercrombie an' Fitch.

— That's the one – in town. They have tha'. Wha' do they want rights for as well?

— You're just bein' thick.

— Ah, I know. Kids are grand. Take them away from their mothers. It's for the best.

— I'm not listenin'.

— An'annyway, it looks like the American election mightn't be goin' ahead now.

— How come?

— It's rainin'.

7-11-12

— Wha' did yeh make of the result last night?

— Glad to see the back of them.

— Who?

— Man City, the fuckin'—

— No, no. I mean in America.

— The presidential yoke?

— Yeah.

— Our man got in.

— Good oul' B'rack.

— I love the way he talks.

— Wha'?

— The way he talks – the speeches, like.

— Is this one o' your Andriy Shevchenko moments?

— Fuck off – no. I'm just sayin'. Him an' Morgan Freeman. An' your man, the dead one. Martin Luther King. They're great fuckin' talkers.

— They're all black.

— That's part of it, yeah. It's the style o' the thing.

— Wha' the fuck are you on?

— No, listen. 'We have picked ourselves up.' He stops an' they cheer. 'We have fought our way back.' Same again. 'An' we *KNOW* in our hearts.' They're goin' fuckin' mad. 'Tha' for the United States of America.' He makes them wait, then, 'The-best-is-yet-to-come.' It's fuckin' brilliant, tha'. 'The-best-is-yet-to-come.'

— It *is* a Shevchenko moment.

— It fuckin' isn't. Not with Michelle beside him.

— Now you're makin' sense.

— Gorgeous.

— Fuckin' gorgeous.

— The election, but. What's a swing state?

— I'm not sure, but you should probably think o' fuckin' movin' to one.

9-11-12

— Are yeh votin' Yes or No tomorrow?

— Well. I had one small doubt, but I think I'm covered.

— Wha'?

— Well, every Stephen's Day I dangle the grandkids by their feet over the side o' the pedestrian bridge in Fairview. It's a family tradition. Hot chocolate after.

— Nice.

— So. My worry was tha' if the thing is passed an' children get their rights, then they'd have the righ' to dangle me.

— It'd take a fair few six-year-olds to hold on to you.

— Tha' was the worry. But I was assured, by a chap handin' out the leaflets, that tha' possibility is covered under existin' weights and measures legislation. The holder of the legs must be four times heavier than the holdee. So I'm grand. An' then as well—

— Wha'?

— I seen tha' prick on the telly.

— Which one?

— The bald fella with the long hair. Yeh know him?

— The oul' 'if-Jesus-had-lived-a-bit-longer' look.

— That's him. He came last in the Eurovision.

— It's some fuckin' achievement.

— Anyway, he made a remark abou' foster-parents. Suggested tha' they're in it for the money. An' I says to myself, tha' cynical cunt would say annythin' for a No vote. So fuck him – I'm votin' Yes.

11

21-11-12

- - - -
  - - -
- - - - - -
— So, look it.
— Wha'?
— We're goin' to have to get past this.
- - Okay.
— I'll say it – I don't mind.
— Okay.
— Just the once.
— Okay.
— An' then we can move on.
— Grand. Go on.
— Righ' – okay. Yeh ready?
— Yeah – go on.
- - - Abortion.
- - -
— Tha' wasn't too bad.
— No.
— We're over the hump.
— Yeah.
— Grand.
- - -
- - - -
- - Is—?
— Yeah?
— Is it okay if we have another pint now?
— Fire away, yeah.
— Thanks.

— See the Pope says there were no donkeys in the stable.

— Rafa Benitez.

— Was he in the fuckin' stable?

— Rafa fuckin' Benitez.

— Good man.

— Rafa fuckin' cuntin' Benitez.

— Get it out o' your system.

— I mean – how can he get away with it?

— Who?

— Tha' Russian—. What's the word for a rich Russian fella – begins with 'o'?

— Cunt.

— How can he just play with my fuckin' heart?

— D'yeh want a hug?

— Fuck off. Look it. I've been followin' Chelsea twenty years longer than I've known my missis.

— That's two fuckin' disasters, so.

— Fuck off. Look. In all the years – all the managers an' tha'. Goin' way back. To the '60s, like. Tommy Docherty, Dave Sexton. I've never liked it when the manager was sacked. Never. But I never felt any hostility towards the new man comin' in. Even tha' fuckin' eejit, Hoddle. But Rafa fuckin' Benitez – ah, fuck. I'll be watchin' them tomorrow—

— Don't watch it.

— I fuckin' have to. An' I'll be shoutin' at the telly – 'Fuck off back to Spain, yeh scouse cunt.' An' yeh know what'll happen?

— Wha'?

— Torres will score two an' the next time I'm down here I'll be callin' him Rafa.

4-12-12

— See Kate Middleton's pregnant.

— Who's the da?

— Ah, stop it now. She's a nice young one.

— Serious. Who is it? I always forget.

— It's – fuck. I forget now, meself. His name, like.

— Just to be clear. She's not the one on *I'm A Fuckin' Celebrity Get Me Ant And Dec Are A Pair O' Twats Out O' Here*?

— No.

— Or the one with the cookery book.

— I don't think so – no.

— Grand. Tha' narrows it down.

— William.

— Wha'?

— That's who's she's married to.

— William who?

— Prince William.

— Okay. An' he's the da, is he?

— Yeah.

— Yeh sure?

— Ah, fuck off now.

— Did yeh never watch *The* fuckin' *Tudors*, did yeh not?

— That's just telly.

— They'd get up on annythin', them royals.

— Annyway. She's pregnant.

— So wha'?

— Ah, lay off.

— I'm serious. So wha'?

— Well, it's just a bit o' good news—

— It isn't news at all. It's only fuckin' gossip.

— Well, d'yeh want to talk abou' tomorrow's Budget instead?

— It might be twins, apparently.

14

— Cos o' the strength o' the mornin' sickness.

— Spot on, yeah.

— How were yeh feelin', yourself, this mornin'?

— Ah Jesus, man – fuckin' triplets. Definitely. All boys.

— Take a look at tha'.

— What is it?

— A property tax voucher.

— A wha'?

— I was listenin' to the news there. The Budget, like. An' they're goin' on abou' the property tax. An' I just thought – Bingo. Last year I bought a goat – online, like.

— For young Damien.

— Exactly, yeah. A stockin' filler. But annyway. I'd actually bought the goat for some family in fuckin' Somalia or somewhere. An' all I got was a voucher an' a picture of a fuckin' goat. You with me?

— Eh—

— So annyway, the oul' brainwave. I get young Damien to give me a hand. I do up a PDF—

— A wha'?

— Stay with me. I bring the memory stick up to the late-night chemist, to the chap at the back who does the photographs. He's got a state-o'-the-art photocopier in there with him. So he does me five thousand copies.

— It's a lovely job. How's it work but?

— This one here, look. For fifty euro. Yeah?

— Yeah.

— Yeh give – whoever – the voucher an' a photograph of the thing you were goin' to give them before they announced the fuckin' property tax.

— Brilliant.

— Two euro a pop, includin' the envelope.

— See the spacer died.

   — Wha' spacer?

   — The *Sky at Night* fella.

   — Bobby Moore.

   — Patrick Moore.

   — That's him, yeah. Did he die?

   — Yeah.

   — That's a bit sad. He was good, wasn't he?

   — Brilliant. Very English as well.

   — How d'yeh mean?

   — Well, like – he'd look into his telescope an' his eyebrows would go mad cos he was so excited abou' all the fuckin' stars an' the planets an' tha'. An' the words—

   — They fuckin' poured out of him.

   — Exactly. It was brilliant. But if he'd been Irish, he'd just've said, So wha'? They're only fuckin' stars. There's no way it would've been the longest-runnin' programme in the history o' television if it'd been Irish.

   — You might be righ'.

   — Think about it. Our attitude is just shite.

   — I remember once, but. He was goin' on abou' how the light from stars took millions o' years to reach here and how the light we saw might be comin' from stars tha' were long dead – cos it took so long, like. An' well—

   — Wha'?

   — Maybe he died years ago an' we're only findin' out about it now.

16-12-12

— Did yeh go past my place on your way?

— I did, yeah.

— Notice annythin'?

— It's still there.

— You'll need to be a bit more fuckin' specific.

— Lovely tree.

— No.

— Big Santy in the garden.

— Union Jack.

— Wha'?

— The flag. Hangin' off the chimney.

— Well, it's fuckin' night-time. So, no, I didn't—. Are yeh serious?

— I am, yeah.

— You've the flag o' Britain on top o' your house?

— Yeah.

- - - Why?

— The Shinners in Belfast voted to get rid of it, off the top o' City Hall – yeah?

— The riots an' tha'.

— Yeah. Except for fifteen days o' the year. So I bought one.

— A Union Jack?

— Off eBay, yeah.

— Okay, grand. Fuckin' why, but?

— Show the cunts it works both ways. I'm hangin' me flag for fifteen days o' the year. Paddy's Day, Easter Monday. All the biggies.

— Why today?

— Excitement. When I opened the package, like. I was straight out to the ladder.

— Jaysis.

— Sure, it's Christmas.

— What abou' Continuity Carl across the way? You're not worried he'll lob a petrol bomb at yis?

— With his one remainin' hand.

— Yeah.

— No. Tha' fucker wouldn't take tha' hand ou' of his tracksuit bottoms for an Ireland free.

22-12-12

— Anny idea wha' you're gettin' for Christmas?

— Bottle o' the Brad Pitt stuff.

— Wha'?

— Inevitable.

— Wha'?

— If it works for Brad, it'll work for me. Slap a bit on after I shave an' I'll be beatin' the women off me.

— Hang on—

— Poor oul' Brad. Angelina's too busy with all them orphans she bought in Somalia.

— Was tha' not Madonna?

— There was a sale. So, annyway, Brad has a shave an' slaps on the Inevitable an' he says, 'I'm just goin' ou' for some milk an' nappies, love,' an' he—

— Yeh missed somethin'.

— Wha'?

— He has a beard.

— So?

— He didn't shave.

— It's only one o' them little Three Musketeers ones—

— It's not aftershave.

— I know – they don't call it aftershave—

— It's not called Inevitable.

— Wha'?

— It's Chanel No. 5.

— I don't give a fuck what it is—. Hang on. The fuckin' perfume?

— Yep.

— Women's perfume?

— Well spotted.

— I never fuckin' noticed. What's tha' dopey cunt doin' on an ad for women's perfume?

— Makin' a few quid.

— For fuck sake. She asked me what I wanted an' I told her a bottle of Inevitable, an' she just smiled an' said Grand.

— Wha' did you get her?

— *FIFA Manager 13.*

31-12-12

— Fiscal cliff.

— He's shite.

— Wha'?!

— He's just copyin' the other fella.

— Wha' the fuck are yeh talkin' about?

— The rapper.

— Wha' rapper?

— Fiscal Cliff.

— There's no fuckin' rapper called—. You're messin', yeh cunt.

— I am, yeah.

— It's serious, but. Isn't it? The fiscal cliff.

— Seems to be.

— How?

— Don't know. Spendin' cuts, deficits – the usual shite.

— America goes into recession.

— An' so do we.

— Wha' the fuck are we in at the moment?

— Exactly. We're already fucked.

— Still though. A crap end to a crap year.

— They're all crap.

— Wha'?

— Every fuckin' year I've lived has been crap.

— Ah now.

— It's all shite.

— Hang on – calm down. The birth of your oldest.

— A great day in the middle of a fuckin' shite year.

— Your youngest.

— My ma died the same day. Fuckin' dreadful.

— Your weddin'.

— I remember half an hour an' the rest o' the year I was hung-over an' out o' work.

— Your first ride.

— Five minutes. The rest o' the '70s were fuckin'
unbearable. An' the fuckin' '80s.

— I'm not listenin'.

— A waste o' time – I'm tellin' yeh. As for the '90s—

— Ah, fuck off.

— Happy New Year.

— Fuck off.

— God, you're fuckin' miserable.

14-1-13

— See the new boss o' the Bank of Ireland is a lighthouse keeper.

— He can't be anny worse than the dozy cunts that've been runnin' it up to now.

— True. Although – did yeh see the ad, did yeh?

— I did, yeah.

— So. You've your man arrivin' at the lighthouse.

— In the pissin' rain, yeah.

— To change the light bulb.

— An' he manages it all righ'.

— It's comfortin' tha', isn't it? Tha' the new boss o' the bank can change a bulb.

— An' he turns on the light as well, don't forget.

— Fair enough – it's a busy day.

— An' the voice is goin', 'We recognise tha' for the last few years the waters have been particularly stormy.'

— Un-fuckin'-believable.

— An' this bit. 'That's why we want – an' need – to renew our commitment to look ou' for you.'

— You know it off by heart.

— I fuckin' do.

— But did you notice his bike?

— Wha'?

— When he's inside in the lighthouse lookin' ou' for us, his bike's outside. Parked against the wall, like.

— Yeah – okay. And?

— The fuckin' eejit forgot to lock it.

— Did he?

— Annyone could fuckin' rob it.

— So it's business as usual at the Bank of Ireland.

— Exactly.

— When was the last time yeh ate a burger?

— Jaysis – I don't know. A good while back. This mornin', I think. Maybe last nigh' – not sure. Why?

— Did yeh not see the fuckin' news before yeh came ou'?

— I did, yeah.

— How they found traces of horse an' pig DNA in beefburgers, in Tesco's an' Dunne's an'—

— So?

— So? Fuckin' so?

— It's still meat.

— But it's not fuckin' beef.

— The beef isn't beef either. I couldn't give a shite. Long as it's not slugs or maggots or eyeballs an' tha'.

— You're fuckin' serious.

— Long as they taste alrigh' – what's the fuckin' fuss?

— Wha' abou' standards?

— This is fuckin' Ireland, bud – cop on.

— So – say—

— Go on. You're goin' to say somethin' stupid.

— Fuck off now, an' listen. Say it was human DNA?

— Grand. It's meat.

— Yeh wouldn't mind eatin' human?

— No. But it depends.

— On wha'?

— Wha' sort o' human it was.

— Wha' d'yeh mean? Not race—

— God, no. No – fuck tha'. No, I could never eat a Man United supporter. It'd make me fuckin' sick.

— I'm with yeh. Or a City fan.

— No meat on those fuckers.

— Or a child.

— Not one o' me own, no.

18-1-13

— You look a bit lost.

— Ah fuck it—

— Wha'?

— She caught me smokin'.

— At home?

— Ou' the back, yeah.

— How long have yeh been off them?

— Ten years – officially.

— Jesus. Wha' did she say?

— I've to go on *Oprah Winfrey*.

— Wha'?!

— She's comin' to the house.

— Hang on – *the* Oprah Winfrey?

— Yeah.

— She's comin' to your fuckin' house?

— To interview me, yeah. To hear me confession.

— Fuck off.

— Don't believe me – I don't give a fuck. She's fuckin' furious.

— Oprah?

— The wife. She's makin' me do the hooverin' before your woman arrives. With her 112 fuckin' questions.

— Will you admit it?

— I will, yeah – no problem. But listen. She – the wife – says it was the most sophisticated, organised and professionalised sneaky smoke in the history of sneaky smokin'.

— She's a way with the fuckin' words.

— Well – between ourselves now – she can fuck off. I'll be tellin' Oprah that all people my age – tha' generation – we all fuckin' smoked. There were East Germans smoked a lot more than me. I was quite conservative. But yeah,

26

I'll admit it. Then I'll be back on the bike – with a bit o' luck.

— Will yeh say you're sorry?

— I will in me fuckin' hole.

— See Heffo died.

— Sad.

— Heffo's Army, wha'.

— Good days.

— Were yeh one of the lads yourself back then?

— No, I wasn't big into the Gaelic at all. But it wasn't tha'. It wasn't the football.

— Wha' d'yeh mean?

— It was the whole Dubs thing. The pride, yeh know. When they started winnin'.

— We were Dubs.

— Exactly. We were Dubs. Against the rest of the country.

— The culchies.

— The kids call them boggers.

— Well, they'll always be culchies in my heart. Especially the Kerrymen.

— No argument. They're the best culchies of the lot.

— I worked with a chap from Kerry. Nice enough fella but I couldn't understand a fuckin' word he said. I'm pretty certain it wasn't English.

— Irish, maybe.

— Maybe, yeah. His sandwiches, righ'? They were so big – he'd lift it to his mouth an' his whole fuckin' head would disappear behind it. Only his fringe, like – hangin' over the edge.

— See they're thinkin' of allowin' drink-drivin' in Kerry?

— Great idea.

— D'yeh think?

— No question. Think of it. Tourism. Telly. You'd come in after a few pints an' there's a programme on called *Drunk Kerry Drivers – Live*. You'd watch it.

— I'd get locked just to watch it.

— See the last o' the Andrews Sisters died.

— Whose sisters?

— The Andrews Sisters. They were singers.

— Oh.

— Durin' the war.

— A bit weird, tha'.

— Wha'?

— They stopped singin' when the war ended. Were they Nazis or somethin'?

— Ah, fuck off. My da loved them.

— Did he?

— He did, yeah – loved them. He was in the RAF.

— Was he?

— He was, yeah. Did I never tell yeh?

— Hang on – your da was fuckin' Biggles?

— Well, there now. There was once – I was a kid, like – an' I ask him what he was in the RAF. An' he looks at me an' he says, 'Well, son, I was a fuckin' air hostess.'

— Brilliant.

— He was great, me da. He was a mechanic.

— Fixed the planes.

— Exactly. But he never mentioned it much. In case some fuckin' eejit called him a Brit an' took a swing at him. But he loved the Andrews Sisters. Had the record.

— Give us one o' their songs.

— There was one abou' sittin' under the apple tree.

— Give us a few bars.

— No – fuck off. Not here.

— Ah, go on. Did he play it a lot?

— He did, yeah. Specially after me ma died.

— Ah shite – sorry.

— No, you're grand – you're grand. It's your round by the way. The barman wants yeh.

4-2-13

— See Richard the Third was found dead in a car park.

— Who?

— Richard the Third.

— Who was he?

— The King of England.

— Wha' happened the fuckin' Queen?

— Before her.

— He was her da?

— I think so, yeah. Grandda maybe. Annyway, they found him.

— They took their fuckin' time.

— Yeah – yeah. I'd like to think that if I got lost my gang'd try a bit fuckin' harder.

— He was probably a bit of a cunt.

— Safe bet. They're all cunts.

— Wha' happened him annyway?

— He couldn't find his car.

— So he just lay down an' fuckin' died?

— Well, like. If you're used to people doin' everythin' for yeh—

— Ah, fuck off.

— I'm only messin'. He was in a fight. Swords an' all.

— The car park was in fuckin' Swords?

— No – the fight. There were swords. He was brutally hacked – accordin' to the English guards.

— How do they know it was him? He must've been there for ages.

— His DNA.

— What about it?

— It was 45 per cent horse.

— Ah well, then he was definitely one o' the British royal family.

— Science is incredible, isn't it?

— Brilliant.

30

— See the Trogg died.

    — I saw tha', yeah. Reg Presley.

    — With a name like tha' he was never goin' to be a plumber, was he?

    — It wasn't his real name.

    — Was it not?

    — No. His real one was Reg Ball.

    — You were a bit of a fan, were yeh?

    —I was, yeah. I was only a kid when 'Wild Thing' came ou'—

    — It made your heart sing.

    — That's the one. One of me brothers had the record an' he left it behind when he got married, so it was always in the house.

    — Great song.

    — Brilliant song. Still.

    — Could you get away with it now?

    — Wha'?

    — Callin' a woman a wild thing.

    — I don't see why not. I called my missis exactly tha' this morning after the news.

    — An' she was grand with it?

    — Fuckin' delighted. I put me arms around her – I was a bit emotional, like. An' I sang it to her.

    — Nice.

    — In the kitchen.

    — An' tell us – without invadin' your privacy. Did it develop into a bit of a Jack Nicholson, Jessica Lange moment? On the table.

    — Not exactly, no. But she put an extra dollop o' jam into me porridge.

    — For fuck sake.

    — Blackcurrant.

    — Nice.

7-2-13

— So. Anglo's gone.

— Liquidated.

— Great fuckin' word.

— But—

— Wha'?

— Is it good news or bad news?

— That's the fuckin' problem, isn't it? We don't really know.

— An' no one else does either. Not one o' those cunts on the telly or the radio has a fuckin' clue.

— 'Cept your man, the economist fella. Constantin.

— Constantin Gurdgiev.

— Him – yeah. He looks like he knows wha' he's on abou'.

— Only because he's the only one tha' doesn't look like he's tryin' to sell yeh his wife or a second-hand Hiace. His face, like.

— Buster Keaton.

— Exactly.

— So, does he think we're any better off?

— I couldn't really understand him. But he said none o' those Anglo season ticket holders—

— Bondholders.

— Yeah. None o' them should've got their money back. They could fuck off with their promissory notes.

— Did he say tha'?

— More or less.

— He's one o' the lads, so. One thing, but.

— Wha'?

— Yeh know the way no one really gives a shite abou' the horse DNA in the burgers?

— Yeah.

— Well, it's the same with this Anglo shite, isn't it? They can't scare us annymore.

— 'Cept Buster.

— Fair enough. He's a bit fuckin' scary.

10-2-13

— What's wrong?

— I stuck twenty euro on a horse.

— An' it lost.

— No, it won.

— Wha'?

— Listen. Me cousin texts me – yesterday. Stick a few quid on Paddy's Boyband, in the four o'clock at Leopardstown. So I do. An' he wins.

— The horse.

— Yes, the fuckin' horse. So. I go into Paddy Power's – just now. An' the young one at the hatch tells me he's disqualified. He failed a fuckin' test.

— Dopin'.

— No. DNA. They found traces of horse DNA.

— In the horse?

— 73 per cent.

— Hang on – fuck off. The horse was only 73 per cent horse?

— Yeah.

— But—. Wha'? 27 per cent of the horse wasn't fuckin' horse?

— Yeah.

— Wha' was it?

— Beef.

— Fuckin' beef?

— Here's me theory, righ'. They've been puttin' horse DNA into the beefburgers, yeah?

— Okay.

— So there's the problem. They need to get rid of the beef they took ou' of the burgers to make room for the horse.

— Hang on—

— So they shove it into the horses.

— Shove?

— Inject – I'd say.

— Fuckin' hell. How can a horse that's more than a quarter cow win a fuckin' race?

— We've been underestimatin' cows for years.

— Are you fuckin' havin' me on? - - - Are yeh?

13-2-13

— Pope's gone.

  — Fuckin' tragic.

  — There's a thing.

  — Wha'?

  — Wha' was his name?

  — Jesus—. I can't remember. I never really got the hang of it.

  — Gas but, isn't it? Can you imagine – back in school, say? Not rememberin' the Pope's name. We'd've been murdered.

  — Shows yeh how times've changed.

  — Gas.

  — An' he resigned. I didn't know they could do tha'.

  — He's frail. I heard a lad on the radio. Why he resigned, like. Wha' d'yeh think tha' means?

  — He's gay.

  — Ah stop it. You're not usin' your imagination.

  — That's wha' she says, at home.

  — Why?

  — We won't go there. He's frail.

  — Yeah. But what's it mean?

  — Go on.

  — Say – tonigh'. We have a few pints more than the normal. How will yeh feel tomorrow?

  — Shite.

  — Grand. An' as well as tha' you'll feel a bit—?

- - - Frail.

  — Good man.

  — So, you're sayin' he drinks.

  — It's a theory.

  — He's one o' the lads.

  — Far-fetched. But is it impossible?

— No.

— After work, like. He puts on jeans an' a jumper.

— An' has a few cans.

— But he can't cope annymore.

— Mass in the mornin's.

— Meetin' African nuns.

— Fuck it, he says.

— In German.

— I'm out o' here.

27-2-13

— See they found traces o' greyhound DNA in the horse meat they've been puttin' in the burgers.

— Borin'.

— Borin'?

— I've moved on.

— Well, before yeh do—

— Go on.

— There was a chap on the radio – a food scientist. An' he says, if yeh handle a piece o' meat you leave traces of your DNA on it.

— So?

— So? For fuck sake – listen. I had a bit o' steak earlier. I handled it an' the missis handled it.

— Why both o' yis?

— We're makin' the dinner together these days. Some shite she read at the dentist's. Adds excitement to the fuckin' marriage.

— How?

— Movin' on. The butcher handled it.

— Wearing the plastic gloves.

— I've no proof o' tha'. He gave the wife a hug before he left the house. You're sittin' up now, yeh cunt.

— I fuckin' am. It's the name of a book, I think.

— Wha'?

— *The Butcher's Wife.*

— I bet it's a good one. Annyway. I had me steak, so I ate the cow, meself, the wife, the butcher, the butcher's wife an' maybe her sister, if the rumours are true. An' that's borin', is it?

— Which sister?

— Does it matter?

— It kind o' does, yeah.

8-3-13

— See the French bird says there's good news on the horizon.

— Wha' French bird?

— Your woman with the scarf. The IMF boss – what's her fuckin' name.

— Madame Lagarde.

— That's the one. She's very happy with us. We've been very good, apparently.

— It's International Women's Day.

— Yeah. So?

— Yeh just called the head of the IMF the French bird.

— She is fuckin' French. Unless she's just messin' Wha' d'yeh think the good news is? She didn't say.

— Yeh can't call the head of the IM fuckin' F a bird.

— Why not? Hang on – I've sussed it. You've done it again, haven't yeh?

— Wha'? No – fuck off.

— Go on, yeh cunt. You've fallen in love with her.

— Fuck off.

— Jesus, every time. A woman in any sort of authority – an' you're fuckin' smitten.

— You're talkin' shite.

— Your woman, Bhutto.

— She was gorgeous.

— Okay.

— An' tragic.

— Yeah, yeah. But Condoleezza?

— She was lonely.

— For fuck sake. An' Hillary?

— She could've done better than Bill.

— Wha' – you?

— No – fuck off. Not necessarily.

— Does your missis know you're in love with half the world's politicians?

— She's gone.

— Fuck – where?

— Chavez's funeral.

— For fuck sake.

— Well, she let me go to Benazir's.

— Fair enough.

— Would you take penalty points for your missis?

— Not 'would', bud. Did.

— Did yeh?

— A few years back. When we went from miles to the other yokes.

— Kilometres.

— Yeah.

— Wha' happened?

— She took the van down to the chipper.

— Why didn't she just walk?

— Big order, an' her back was at her. So anyway, a couple o' Gardas seen her burnin' the rubber on the way back. An' they order her to stop. But she panics – so she said. The priority was to get the chips home.

— The maternal instinct.

— Yeah, yeah. So the fuckin' Guards ring the bell—

— Oh fuck.

— An' she said I'd been the one drivin'.

— Did they believe her?

— No.

— Where were you?

— Out the back. So, annyway. The day we're up in the district court, she drags me down to the fuckin' hairdresser. Gay Larry – d'yeh know him?

— I do, yeah.

— A fuckin' genius. By the time he's finished with us we're fuckin' twins. An' we stand side by side in the court, same hair, an' in our leisure gear, yeh know. An' the judge – he just gives up.

— Brilliant.

— But—

— Wha'?

— He fuckin' winked at me.
— The cunt.
— Fuckin' ugly as well.

13-3-13

— He isn't black.

   — Who? Stevie Wonder?

   — The Pope.

   — The fuckin' Pope?

   — He isn't black.

   — Is he – like – is he supposed to be?

   — Yeah.

   — Well, he's only new. Give him a chance. What's the problem?

   — Cheltenham.

   — Wha'?

   — I was in Paddy Power's earlier – stuck a tenner on Back In Focus in the openin' race.

   — Hang on – he won.

   — Yeah, but—

   — Wha'?

   — It was a double. Back In Focus to win the National Hunt Chase an' a black pope by the end of the day. Hundred to one.

   — Fuckin' hell. An' Black Pope wasn't a horse?

   — No. Black Pope was a black fuckin' pope. So, like – I'm watchin' it on telly. White smoke. Fuckin' great – he's elected today. Then they're sayin' – the fuckin' experts – they're saying he'll be Italian cos the election was so fast. An' I'm thinkin' unless they've elected Mario Balotelli I'm fucked. But then they announce he's from Argentina. An' I get a bit giddy. I kind o' mix up Argentina an' Brazil. There's loads o' black Brazilian footballers, so I'm still in with a chance. But then this white prick walks out onto the balcony.

   — Pope Frankie.

   — The bastard.

— My young one is in trouble. An' her fella.

— Ah, no.

— The mortgage, yeh know.

— They can't handle it?

— They're fucked, God love them. They've been into the bank an' tha', to try an' sort somethin'. But—

— No joy?

— It's fuckin' madness. Her fella was in the chipper last nigh'. He gives his order, then sees the onion rings an' he tells Gaddafi he'll have one. Then someone taps him on the shoulder an' he turns, and this cunt in the queue says, 'You can't have the onion ring.'

— Fuck off.

— That's exactly wha' my young one's fella says. An' your man, the other fella, takes out his ID an' flashes it. Bank of Ireland.

— No!

— An' he proceeds to tell him he can have the chips – but only once a month. An' he can't have the onion ring. Ever. Or until the mortgage is fully paid.

— Wha' did your lad say?

— He said the onion ring was one of his daily five an' the prick from the bank could fuck off with himself.

— Wha' then?

— The bank prick follows him home. Shouts in the letterbox, 'Hope that's not Sky Sports you're watchin'!'

— It's fuckin' harassment.

— It's the future.

8-4-13

— Jesus. It's like New Year's in here.

— An' it's only a fuckin' Monday. He wouldn't take money for the pints.

— Who wouldn't?

— The miserable cunt tha' owns this dump. The pints are for nothin' till closin'. So he says.

— Fuckin' hell. It's a pity Thatcher couldn't die every fuckin' day.

— We'll make the most of this one, so.

— I never called a woman a cunt in me life.

— Except Thatcher.

— You're the same?

— I am. Yeh know what I hated most about her?

— I won't bother guessin'.

— She made me think like a Provo.

— Wha'?

— Every time she opened her mouth about Ireland. With her 'Out, out, out'. Remember?

— I fuckin' do.

— An' durin' the hunger strikes. Every time she spoke. She hated us.

— I always thought – she couldn't figure out tha' we weren't British. She was a bit thick.

— You're probably righ'. Anyway—

— She's gone.

— Cheers.

— Cheers. Come here, but. Who d'yeh think she's sittin' beside in hell?

— Some fucker with an accordion.

— Playin' 'Kevin Barry'.

— Out of tune.

— For all fuckin' eternity.

— Longer.

14-4-13

— Anny news?

— It's war.

— Oh, fuck. Korea?

— Fuck Korea. At home – in the house, like. Herself.

— Hate tha'. What's the story?

— She's goin' across to Thatcher's funeral.

— Wha'?!

— I know – I fuckin' know. I can't fuckin' believe it. She says – listen to this. She says she's always modelled herself on Thatcher.

— Fuckin' hell. Did you ever notice?

— Fuck, no – Jaysis, no. No, no. She's lovely, sure. Isn't she?

— Go on.

— Sure, she collected for the miners back in the day, an' she named the fuckin' dog Las Malvinas. But there's no remindin' her. She's on the Holyhead boat tomorrow.

— Jesus—

— It's un-fuckin'-believable. So I went on the counter-attack, o' course.

— Thatcher-style.

— Fuck off. I was a bit mean, like. I told her I'd never seen a picture o' Thatcher sittin' up in the bed in a pink onesie, playin' Texas holdem on her grandson's tablet.

— An' wha' did she say?

— The usual. An' fair enough. But then – I'm not proud o' this – I called her a scanger. I just whispered it, like.

— Oh, boy. What did she say then?

— The scanger's not for turnin'.

46

26-4-13

— Did yeh ever bite anyone?

— God, yeah.

— Wha'?

— Loads o' times.

— Not when you were a baby, like.

— I know, yeah. I know exactly wha' you're at. Yeh want me to join the witch-hunt against poor Luis Suárez.

— But—

— Just cos he bit a Serb in the penalty area.

— Fuck off a minute. I'm serious.

— So am I. So sit back there, yeh cunt, an' I'll tell yeh the problem. The root of it, like. An' not just scapegoatin' fuckin' Suárez.

— Okay. Go on.

— Christianity.

— Wha'?

— Fuckin' Christianity. I'm tellin' yeh. All these fuckin' players – you've seen them. They bless themselves goin' on the pitch, or look up to the sky – talkin' to God, like. An' the first thing they do is rake their studs down some poor fucker's shins. Or they dive – they hit the deck like they're bein' ridden by a bear. But it's grand, because they're Christians an' they talk to God an' he's obviously told them they can kick an' cheat an' pull jerseys as much as they like. They're fuckin' crusaders. An' Suárez was just showin' God how much he loved him.

— By bitin' Ivanovic?

— Exactly. It was fuckin' heroic.

1-5-13

— See they're talkin' about legislatin' for the right to an abortion in the event of your team bein' relegated.

— Fuck off – you're sick.

— Serious. I heard it on the radio – I think I did, annyway.

— Fuck off.

— But it has to be actual relegation, not just fear o' relegation – or the *ideation* o' relegation.

— I'm not listenin'.

— An' it'll have to go before a panel of three people. Two doctors – an obstetrician, like, an' a psychiatrist. An' one o' the lads from *Match of the Day*.

— Fuck off.

— So I heard. If there's a genuine prospect of the team bein' relegated an' the woman wants an abortion, the HSE will call in Alan Shearer—

— Fuckin' Shearer?!

— Or Dion Dublin.

— Ah, for fuck sake. It's fuckin' typical. What's wrong with one of our own punters?

— So. If I'm right—. You think it's okay for a woman to have an abortion if she gets the all-clear from Brian Kerr or Kenny Cunningham.

— Yeah – no. Fuck off.

— Or Lawrenson.

— Fuck off.

— Or Roy Keane.

— She'd listen to Roy.

— See he's gone.

— Jimmy Tarbuck?

— Fuck off – Sir Alex.

— An' for the same reason.

— Don't start now.

— Why d'yeh think he held on to Giggs and fuckin' Scholes for so long?

— You're fuckin' sick.

— Buyin' their silence. They were only little lads when they were forced to join tha' fuckin' club. Fuckin' kidnapped they were.

— I'm not listenin'.

— On their way to Chelsea.

— Wake me up when you're done.

— An' poor little Beckham as well. But Posh rescued him, thank God.

— Are yeh finished?

— Go on.

— It's the end of an era.

— Is tha' the best yeh can do?

— Well, it fuckin' is.

— Okay – grand. What is a fuckin' era, annyway?

— I don't know. A long time – ages – fuck off.

— Why's he leavin'?

— His hip.

— His fuckin' hip?

— He's havin' it replaced.

— Why can't he fuckin' limp like the rest of us? An' who's replacin' him?

— Mourinho.

— Wha'?! José? Fuck off. He's comin' back to us.

— Not accordin' to the bookies.

— Fuck the bookies. Tell yeh wha' – Sir Alex can have my hip. If it'll make him change his mind. D'yeh have a saw on yeh?

— So. Beckham retired.

— Tha' cunt retired years ago.

— Ah, for fuck sake – relax. Just accept it. He was a great player.

— He wasn't great. He was okay for a couple o' years. Before he met Spice Rack or wha'ever her fuckin' name is.

— God, you're a fuckin' eejit.

— An' I'll tell yeh exactly why he retired.

— G'wan. Why?

— To upstage Angelina.

— Wha'?!

— They couldn't cope – him an' Posh – with all the attention she was gettin' an' all the praise. An' Posh didn't have an illness or a condition of her own to announce, cancer or depression or a second hole in her arse or annythin'. So he says, 'Fuck it, love, I'll announce me retirement.'

— Actually. You're probably righ'.

— I'm definitely righ'.

— Would you tattoo your kids' names on the back of your neck?

— They wouldn't fit.

— I suppose it wouldn't be too bad if the name was Romeo or Brooklyn. But your man over there – Badger.

— What abou' him?

— The tattoo.

— Where?

— On the back of his fuckin' neck

— That's not a tattoo. That's just dirt.

— But look – it says 'John Paul'.

— Coincidence.

— Fuck off.

— An' annyway, it's spelt wrong – look. 'John Pal'.

— Were yeh ever breathalysed?

— Yeah.

— Did yeh pass it?

— No – failed. Fuckin' miserably. But I wasn't drivin'.

— Wha'?

— I wasn't even in a fuckin' car.

— Wha'?!

— I was walkin' home – from here. An' I swerved into the wrong garden an' up to the wrong fuckin' door. An', like, the key wouldn't turn for me. I was so locked, it never occurred to me that I was tryin' to get into the wrong house.

— Whose gaff was it?

— Widow McCarthy's.

— She's not a widow.

— Married to tha' cunt, she might as well be. Annyway, she phoned the Guards. An' that's how they found me – with me key in your woman's lock.

— But yeh weren't in a car.

— No. But the Guard says if I'd been drivin' and I'd taken a wrong turn like tha', I'd've killed meself. An' he breathalysed me, to prove his point.

— Fuckin' eejit.

— Ah, he was grand.

— But – come here. Alan Shatter.

— An' his fuckin' asthma.

— I had asthma – when I was younger, like. An' if I couldn't've done a breathalyser, I'd've either been on me way to A&E or fuckin' dead.

— So, he's lyin' through his arse.

— He can manage tha'. His arse doesn't have asthma.

3-6-13

— What's wrong?

— Nothin'.

— Is someone after dyin'?

— No.

— Well, there's something wrong with yeh. I can tell. Come on, ou' with it.

— Well—

— Yeah?

— Mourinho's back.

— I know. I expected you to be dancin' on the fuckin' counter.

— Well, I'm not.

— But you like Mourinho.

— I fuckin' love Mourinho.

— So, what's the problem?

— Well. I made a pact.

— With the fuckin' devil?

— No. God.

— Mourinho?

— No, the other one. The hairy one, like – the real one, I suppose you'd call him.

— Just – hang on. Just so I'm clear here. You made a pact with God.

— Yeah.

— Do you even believe in God?

— Not really. But – I don't know. I kind o' do.

— Wha' was the pact?

— I'd give up the drink if Mourinho went back to Chelsea.

— For fuck sake. When?

— At me cousin's funeral there, a month ago. In the

church. On me knees, like. I said, I might as well give it a go while I'm down here.

— But, look it, Mourinho was on his way long before tha'.

— Ah, I know.

— An' did God actually answer yeh?

— Not really.

— Annythin' in writin'?

— No.

— Fuck'm, so. You'll have a pint.

— Okay. Grand. Yeah. Thanks.

9-6-13

— Poor oul' Mandela.

— Yeah.

— He's on the way ou'.

— D'yeh know wha', but? He should never've left the Four Tops.

— Fuck off now – just fuck off.

— Okay – sorry. Sorry.

— Okay. D'yeh remember the time he was in town? He was gettin' the freedom o' the city or somethin'.

— Same day the Irish team came home from the World Cup. Italia '90.

— That's righ'. You were with me, yeah?

— Yeah, 'course. We'd most o' the kids with us.

— The ones tha' were born.

— Some fuckin' day.

— I had two o' mine on me shoulders. All fuckin' day. I don't think I ever recovered.

— Great day, but.

— Brilliant. Seein' him. My kids still remember it.

— Good to have done it, so. Gone in, like.

— 'Ooh aah, Paul McGrath's da'. D'yeh remember?

— Brilliant.

— An' him walkin' out o' jail. D'yeh remember tha'?

— Amazin'.

— The dignity, like.

— My cousin. Danno. A mad cunt. He was up in court. Did I ever tell yeh this?

— When was this?

— 'Bout the same time – back then. Anyway, the judge says to him, 'Why did yeh rob the bookie's?' An' Danno says back, 'So I can walk out o' jail like Nelson Mandela.'

— See Tony Soprano died.

  — Sad, tha'.

  — Only a young fella really.

  — Fifty-one.

  — Frightenin' – a bit. Isn't it?

  — Yeah. He was fuckin' brilliant but, wasn't he?

  — Amazin'. *The Sopranos* was the first television series I watched. As an adult, like.

  — I know wha' yeh mean.

  — The other shite was on but I never really watched any of it. *Dallas* an' all tha'. Fuckin' J.R. an' Bobby an' John Boy.

  — Tha' was *The Waltons*.

  — Doesn't matter – same fuckin' shite. An' the soaps were no better.

  — Then Tony arrived.

  — There were times I'd be lookin' at his face an' I'd know wha' he was thinkin'.

  — Cos he was a man.

  — Real, yeah.

  — One o' the lads.

  — Wouldn't go tha' far. Great actor, but.

  — Brilliant. It's been a shite week, hasn't it?

  — They're all shite. What else happened?

  — Well, Michelle Obama. Goin' for a pint with fuckin' Bono. Wha' the fuck was she at?

  — She could've come here.

  — Exactly. Instead she had to listen to tha' prick scutterin' on abou' global poverty an' himself.

  — Her loss.

  — Big time. Yeh know what's tragic about it?

  — Wha'?

— She went back to America without ever havin' tasted Tayto.

— Tony would've liked Tayto.

— He would.

25-6-13

— The Anglo tapes, wha'.

— Don't get me fuckin' started.

— I keep remindin' meself tha' it happened five years ago.

— But it doesn't help, sure it doesn't?

— No.

— 'Get the money in, get the fuckin' money in.'

— Our money.

— Yeah.

— Laughin' at us, they were.

— Bastards.

— If it'd been us – people like us. Lyin' through our arses, commitin' fraud an' tha' – we'd be in the Joy now.

— We went to the wrong school.

— But we paid the fuckin' bill. It's sickenin'. Jesus, man, my young one was cryin' last nigh' – she was askin' us for the money to buy shoes for little Caitlin – the gran'daughter, like. For fuck sake.

— Your man who reported it – Paul Williams.

— He's good, yeah.

— He usually does the gangland guys, doesn't he?

— Yeah.

— An' he always uses their names – The General an' The Monk an' tha'.

— Why doesn't he do the same now?

— Yeah, exactly.

— Which one is the laugher?

— Bowe – I think.

— John 'The Hyena' Bowe.

— Not bad – a bit gentle.

— The Fuckin' Hyena.

— Better. What abou' Fitzpatrick?

— Peter 'The Thick-Lookin' Dopey Fuck' Fitzpatrick.
— Tha' captures the man alrigh'. An' Drumm?
— David 'The Cunt' Drumm.
— Put it on his fuckin' birth cert.

— The fuckin' weather.

— What about it?

— The heat.

— It's not tha' bad.

— This is fuckin' Ireland. It's unnatural. It's – your man said it on the radio. It's an absolute drought.

— It hasn't rained for two weeks. So wha'?

— Well, it must be affectin' you. You've taken your hoodie off.

— That's nothin' to do with the weather. It's a security measure.

— Wha'?!

— I took it off in case some prick decides to shoot me when I'm walkin' past his house. D'yeh remember 1976, do yeh?

— I do, yeah.

— Tha' was weather.

— Un-fuckin'-believable.

— Our dog died o' the heat tha' summer.

— Ah.

— An' we didn't notice till October.

— What abou' the stink?

— We thought it was me da.

— Fuck off – you're messin' again. One thing, but.

— Wha'?

— The colour of the grass. With the heat an' tha'. And Ireland is famous for bein' green. We even have the four green fields – the provinces, like. An' all those republicans fightin' an' dyin' for the four green fields.

— Go on.

— Well, would they have got as worked up if the fields had been brown?

— What're yeh sayin'? We'd still be part o' the British Empire if the weather had been better?

— It's just a thought.

— See she had the baby.

— Who – the big girl from Paddy Power's?

— No. Kate Middleton.

— Who?

— Ah, don't fuckin' start again – pretendin' yeh don't know.

— She's the Queen's cousin or somethin', is she? I get mixed up – I don't give much of a shite.

— She's the Queen's granddaughter-in-law.

— For fuck sake – draw me a fuckin' diagram.

— I don't give much of a shite either, to be honest with yeh.

— Boy or girl?

— Stop fuckin' pretendin'.

— What'll they call him?

— It'll be announced in due course.

— Wha' they should do – if they'd anny imagination or guts . . .

— Wha'?

— Did yeh see the YouTube tha' was doin' the rounds a few weeks back? The missis showed it to me. The fuckin' eejit talkin' to the other pair o' fuckin' eejits abou' how she judges kids by their names.

— Seen it, yeah.

— The fuckin' head on her. Annyway, she objected to Chantelle an' – was it Tyler?

— Think so.

— That's wha' they should call him, so. Tyler. Show solidarity with their people. For once.

— Prince Tyler?

— Why not? The first royal rapper.

— King Tyler.

— The First.

— Or Jamal.

— Jamal the First? Sounds too like a pope. The fuckin'
Orangemen would be riotin' again.

— See Pat Kenny's gone.

— To Celtic?

— Wha'?

— Has he gone to Celtic?

— Fuckin' who?

— Kenny. The young lad tha' plays for Home Farm. Celtic and Colchester were lookin' at him an'—

— Pat Kenny. From RTE.

— What about him?

— He's gone.

— 'Course he's gone. It's the summer. They all fuck off for the summer in tha' place.

— No—

— Replaced by even bigger fuckin' eejits than themselves.

— No—

— Even the news. Kids from Transition Year do the reportin' an' tha'. Little fellas an' girls standin' on boxes so their faces can reach the camera.

— Will yeh fuckin' listen—

— While the other red-faced fuckin' wasters get the same holidays as the teachers they're all married to an' fuck off to France an' Donegal.

— He's fuckin' gone, I'm tellin' yeh!

— Who?

— Kenny! He's gone. For good.

— For ever, like?

— Yeah.

— Did he bring Joe Duffy with him, did he?

— Not as far as I know.

— So. Just to be clear. Pat Kenny doesn't work for RTE anymore.

— No.

— Well, my God. Where's he gone?

— Newstalk.

— An' come here. Seriously. Are we supposed to give a fuck?

— Yeah.

— But do we?

— No.

— No, we don't.

14-8-13

— Thirty-five grand.

— What about it?

— It'd buy yeh a lot of gargle.

— It fuckin' would.

— Thirty-five thousand cans of Dutch Gold. Just for example.

— Fuck – I'm not sure that's an attractive thought annymore.

— I'm just givin' yeh a simple picture. An idea of the scale o' the thing.

— You're talkin' about the amount o' booze tha' got delivered to the Garda station in Belmullet.

— In 2007 – yeah.

— Who gave it to them again?

— Shell – or some gang o' cunts workin' for Shell.

— The Garda inquiry said there was no evidence.

— 'Course not. They fuckin' drank it, didn't they?

— Wha' did they do with the empties?

— Threw them in the fuckin' sea on their way to hammerin' the heads off the protesters.

— Tha' makes sense.

— It's efficient. But yeh know the really mad thing about it?

— Wha'?

— There was only ten Guards in the station.

— That's, like, three an' a half thousands' worth of drink per pig.

— Yep.

— Does tha' include mixers?

— Good question.

— Or crisps an' nuts.

— I know wha' yeh mean. Accessories, like.

— Were yeh ever in Belmullet?

— No – thank fuck.

— Yeh'd need a lot o' free jar to survive a year in tha' fuckin' kip.

20-8-13

— See Elmore Leonard died.

— The singer?

— The writer.

— Which one was he?

— American, brilliant – *Get Shorty*.

— Was tha' him?

— Yeah. Look at me.

— Wha'?

— He wrote loads o' them. Look at me.

— Wha'?

— *Out o' Sight, Jackie Brown, Rum Punch, Killshot*. Look at me.

— I am lookin' at you. Why d'yeh keep fuckin' sayin' tha'?

— It's a quote.

— Wha'?

— It's a line. John Travolta says it.

— In *Get Shorty*.

— Yeah – good. Yeh know it.

— I do, yeah. 'Course. An' I'm goin' to make an educated guess here. Look at me.

— Wha'?

— I bet it's the only line yeh remember from the fuckin' fillum.

— No, it isn't.

— Go on, so. Give us one.

— Fuck off.

— There. I knew it – yeh cunt.

— Wha'?

— Yeh couldn't think of another line.

— I just did.

— Wha'?

— Fuck off.

— Tha' doesn't count. Tha' line is in nearly every fillum worth watchin' tha' was ever made. *Taxi Driver, The Godfather, Adam an' Paul, Bambi*—

— Fuckin' *Bambi*?!

— The rabbit says it, if you're listenin' carefully – when the young prince's birth is announced.

— Fuck off.

— He's a bit of a Shinner, tha' rabbit.

— Look at me.

— Wha'?

— It's your round.

24-8-13

— D'yeh remember 'Kitty Ricketts'?

— I fuckin' married her.

— The song.

— The song, the attitude, the whole fuckin' shebang.

— The song – stop messin'. Yeh know what I fuckin' mean.

— I do, yeah.

— You remember it.

— Yeah.

— It was brilliant, wasn't it?

— Yeah – brilliant. There were great songs back then.

— Great gigs as well.

— Yeah, yeah. The Blades, The Atrix.

— The Radiators from Space.

— Songs about Dublin.

— Made us proud, didn't it?

— Still does.

— The fella tha' wrote tha' one, 'Kitty Ricketts'.

— Philip Chevron – yeah.

— There's a testimonial for him tonigh'.

— Football?

— In the Olympia.

— Football in the Olympia? Fuckin' brilliant. The Radiators from Space versus A Republic of Ireland Eleven – from space.

— Niall Quinn up in the gods.

— His natural fuckin' habitat.

— Eamon Dunphy on drums.

— Tha' makes sense.

— Philip Chevron on the left wing.

— With his mazy runs an' silky skills. Slashin' at his opponents' shins with his guitar.

— He isn't well.

— Yeah.

— Yeh know wha' tha' means – 'isn't well'? For men our age, like.

— I do – yeah.

— Okay.

— Chevron, but. What sort of a name is tha'?

— It's Irish. He dropped the O.

— O'Chevron?

— Exactly. It means son of the unfortunate fucker who couldn't get the odds together to emigrate.

— Here, look it. We don't normally do this. But we'll lift the glass for Philip, will we?

— No – we won't.

— Why not?

— Cos punks don't do tha' shite.

28-8-13

— Could you ever see the Irish Army usin' chemical weapons?

— Well, I could see them goin' into Limerick with a bottle o' Harpic.

— Seriously.

— Why?

— Well – like. The Syrians gassin' their own people.

— Ah, fuck off. Is this one o' those 'we're nicer than the Arabs' conversations?

— No—.

— Cos we're not.

— I know. Although our music's better.

— Not by much.

— Okay. But the gassin' an' tha'. An' the Yanks an' the Brits plannin' on—

— The French as well.

— Never mind the French. They're all mouth, those fuckers. But do none of them have kids or mas or – just, families?

— People they love.

— Exactly. Have they no fuckin' imaginations?

— I nearly gassed the kids once.

— I'm serious.

— I know. They'll tell us they're doin' it for the good of the world but wha' they'll actually be doin' is destroyin' families.

— That's it – it's desperate. If they – Obama an' Cameron an' the headbangers – if they'd think of a great family moment, yeh know, everyone laughin' or something, before they do—. D'yeh know what it is? I'm scared.

— I know wha' yeh mean.

— Do yeh?

— I think so.

72

— See Seamus Heaney died.

— Saw tha'. Sad.

— Did yeh ever meet him?

— Don't be fuckin' thick. Where would I have met Seamus Heaney?

— That's the thing, but. He looked like someone yeh'd know.

— I know wha' yeh mean – the eyebrows an' tha'.

— He always looked like he liked laughin'.

— One o' the lads.

— Except for the fuckin' poetry.

— Wha' would possess a man like tha' to throw his life away on poetry?

— Exactly.

— Although, fair enough – he won the Nobel Prize for it.

— He'd probably have won it annyway.

— For wha' – for fuck sake?

— I don't know. Football, plumbin' – annythin'. Tha' was wha' was special about him. He was brilliant but he looked like he came from around the corner. The poetry, but.

— I feel a confession comin' on.

— I was givin' one o' the grandkids a hand with the homework.

— Go on.

— She had to write about one of his poems. 'Mid-Term Break', it's called.

— Yeah, go on.

— Well, it was fuckin' unbelievable. Just shatterin' – brilliant. About a child's funeral.

— 'A four foot box, a foot for every year.'

— You read it as well.

— You're not the only man in the shop with grandkids.

10-9-13

— See fruit's bad for yeh.

    — I always said it.

    — All tha' one-in-five bolloxology.

    — Fuckin' scientists – they're fuckin' eejits. How could fuckin' kiwis be good for yeh?

    — She's fuckin' furious – at home. She's thinkin' o' suin'.

    — Suin' who?

    — Fuckin' everyone – far as I can make ou'. Says she's suffered permanent spinal damage carryin' all them bananas home from SuperValu.

    — So – she's suin' Africa? The country of origin, like?

    — Africa's not a country – strictly speakin'.

    — Okay—

    — An' in fairness to the Africans, I don't think they came up with this one-in-five shite. They'd have different priorities, I'd say. I think what's really got her goat is the fact tha' she can't claim tha' the blackcurrant in her rum an' black is one of her daily five. She'll have to replace it with celery or broccoli or somethin'.

    — Vegetables are still officially healthy, are they?

    — For the time bein'.

    — I hate them.

    — Yeah. Little green cunts.

    — Useless.

    — It's gas but, isn't it? How we get suckered in. Some prick in a white coat says if you eat all o' your peas Gina Lollobrigida will sit on your face.

    — An' we fall for it.

    — Every fuckin' time.

— So Trap's gone.

    — He was never here.

    — Ah now, that's a bit fuckin' harsh.

    — I'm only statin' a fact. His interpreter—

    — Manuela Spinelli.

    — Exactly. Yeh know the way she stood beside him, noddin' at everythin' he said—

    — It was kind o' sexy.

    — It fuckin' was. Exactly wha' yeh want in a woman. Anyway. The very first press conference, when he got the job, like. He says somethin' in Italian. An' she's noddin' away but you can see it in her eyes.

    — Wha'?

    — Panic.

    — Okay. Why?

    — Cos he thinks he's in Iceland.

    — Wha'?!

    — He thinks he's the new manager of Iceland. Tha' he's in Copenhagen.

    — Reykjavik.

    — Exactly.

    — Fuck off.

    — I'm serious – you fuck off. Look at it on YouTube. She decides – yeh can see it clearly, in her eyes, like – she decides not to give the game away, and she starts goin' on about how he's lookin' forward to workin' with the Irish lads, when he's actually sayin' he's a big fan o' Björk an' he can't wait to see the fuckin' volcanoes.

    — Fuckin' hell.

    — An' she's been at it ever since. Basically.

    — She's – Jesus. Did she choose the teams as well?

    — Someone had to.

17-9-13

— D'yeh think there'll ever be a mad fella with a gun in Ireland like they have them in America?

— Did yeh miss the fuckin' Troubles?

— Yeh know what I mean, but.

— The country's full o' mad cunts with guns. They're always shootin' one another.

— Yeah – one another. The drug fellas an' tha'. But that's just business, isn't it?

— S'pose.

— They're only a bit mad. Wha' they are is cold-blooded businessmen an' the madness is actually an asset. It's wha' you'd be lookin' for in the job interview, like. 'Would yeh work well as part of a team?' 'I'd shoot the fuckin' team.' 'You're in.'

— Okay.

— But the Americans. Like the latest one – a Buddhist with a history o' violence. Yeh couldn't make it up.

— Stop there now. Your man over there – don't fuckin' look!

— Tonto?

— Yeah – Tonto. He's a fuckin' Buddhist.

— Is he?

— Kind of a Catholic Buddhist, but yeah. An' he has a history of violence. An' here's the point. He's still violent. He'd kill us all now, except – why?

— He doesn't want to be barred.

— And?

— He doesn't have a gun.

— Exactly. There's mad fellas everywhere but in America they give them guns.

4-10-13

— See Stephen Ireland's granny died.

— About fuckin' time.

— Jesus, man. That's fuckin' harsh.

— Yeah – okay. I'm sorry for her troubles.

— She's dead.

— Grand. An' it's sad. But it can't've been easy bein' that prick's granny. Sure, he announced she died – how long ago?

— Six years.

— Is it six?

— Yeah.

— Where did they fuckin' go?

— Incredible, isn't it? I can't even remember now why exactly he said she'd died.

— Did he not say tha' more than one granny died?

— A selection of them, yeah. They all denied it.

— Some fuckin' tulip. Imagine not playin' for your country.

— I've never played for me country, so I find it easy to imagine.

— Yeh know what I mean. You get the call—

— At my age?

— No, listen—

— I was always shite at football.

— Just listen. Yeh get the call. No. One of your grandkids – a few years down the line – gets called up to play for Ireland.

— Okay.

— You'd be chuffed.

— Oh yeah.

— But he says he can't play cos his grandda's after dyin'.

— Tha' would be me, would it?

— Yeah.

— An' I wouldn't be dead.

— No.

— I think I'd see the funny side.

— Would yeh, but?

— No.

— See Dublin is the twentieth most reputable city in the world.

— Tha' right? What's above us? Baghdad, Limerick, the other African one – what's it? – Kajagoogoo. An' Damascus. Am I righ'?

— No, you're way off. It's based on reputation.

— Yeah.

— Good reputation.

— Good?

— Yeah.

— I think that's the first time I've ever heard 'good' go beside 'reputation'. I remember, this cunt of a Christian Brother – this was me first day in secondary school – he grabbed me by the hair beside me ear an' he said he'd heard I had a reputation an', I'll tell yeh, it wasn't a fuckin' compliment. There was nothin' good about it. Stamped me for life, it did.

— Well—

— The wife even hesitated when the fuckin' priest asked her if she wanted me to be her lawfully wedded husband.

— Did she?

— She looked at the best man – my fuckin' best man – an' he nodded, an' then she said, 'I do.' It was touch an' go, but.

— Who was the best man?

— That's a different story. But these fuckin' polls. They're all me hole, aren't they?

— Hang on.

— Wha'?

— I was your best man.

— No, yeh weren't. Were yeh?

— Think so.

— Fuck. Wha' weddin' am I rememberin' then?

79

— Wha' colour are your kids' eyes?

— Ah Jesus. Is this me local or *University Challenge*?

— Okay. An easier one. How many kids have yeh? Is it the four?

— Think so, yeah. I get them confused with the grandkids.

— Same here. But you've four, yeah?

— Yeah.

— Grand. Movin' on, so. Eye colour?

— Okay. Righ'. There's three blues, like herself, an' a brown.

— One brown?

— One kid, two fuckin' eyes – both brown.

— Okay. Say the Guards came into your house an' took him away cos one o' your neighbours said he looked nothin' like the other kids.

— Wha' neighbour?

— Don't worry about the fuckin' neighbour. Stay with me. You'd have to show proof tha' he was yours – a DNA test an' tha'. An' you'd be the first item on the mornin' news an' the RTE crime correspondent would be there, even though no crime was committed. It'd be fuckin' appallin'.

— Yeah, but the blue-eyed kid in Greece—

— That's the thing, but. Here, like. In fuckin' Ireland. A blue-eyed kid in among the dark eyes. A little angel in with the gyppos. Must be stolen. But a dark-eyed kid in among all the fair hair? Where's the fuckin' crime correspondent then?

— At home.

27-10-13

— See Lou Reed died.

— Wha'?

— Lou Reed.

— He's after dyin'?

— Yeah.

— He can't've.

— I know wha' yeh mean. But he has.

— But – he – ah, fuck it.

— Sorry.

— There are – listen. There are the ones tha' die young—

— Like Hendrix.

— Yeah. Amy Winehouse an' tha' An' there are the ones tha' don't die. Ever.

— Keith Richards.

— Exactly. An' Iggy Pop.

— An' Lou.

— You're positive about this now?

— Yeah. He's definitely dead. It was in the news.

— Fuck.

— He was good.

— He was fuckin' brilliant. Remember tha' one, 'Vicious'?

— I do, yeah.

— I smashed me ankle cos o' tha' song.

— How come?

— Dancin'. Fell off me fuckin' platforms.

— Yeh wore platforms?

— Once. Bought the fuckin' things tha' day. Executin' one o' me dance moves on the kitchen floor – an' gone. Jesus, m'n, the fuckin' pain. It still gives me grief when the weather's damp.

— Great song, but.

— No argument. Tha' whole album, *Transformer* – one o' the best.

— 'Walk on the Wild Side' – he shaved his legs an' became a she.'

— When yeh hear words like tha', when you're a teenager. In the early 70s, like.

— Did yeh ever shave your legs?

— No. Decided against.

— Same here. How's the ankle?

— Fuckin' killin' me.

— See the chap with no arms was convicted for arms possession.

— Wha' the fuck are you on about now?

— It was in the news. The body parts they found in Meath. An arm found in the woods an' the torso in the river an' tha'.

— What exactly is a fuckin' torso, an'annyway?

— I know what yeh mean – where does it start an' end. Annyway, they named the fella that owned the various bits – the Guards did. They knew him, an' he had a prior conviction for arms possession. It'd make yeh laugh.

— No.

— No. You're probably righ'. It's ironic, but.

— Everythin's fuckin' ironic. Isn't it? These days. Do we even know what it fuckin' means?

— Only kind of.

— I forgot me keys – oooooh, that's fuckin' ironic.

— Calm down, for fuck sake. Yeh goin' home early to watch *Love/Hate*?

— Fuckin' sure. Have to watch it live.

— Best thing ever on Irish telly.

— No argument. Come here, they'll probably find an arm that used to be owned by a fella tha' did time for arms possession.

— That'd be a bit far-fetched.

— True. But the lads diggin' up your man's dead ma last week was brilliant, wasn't it?

— Class.

— See Yasser Arafat was poisoned.

   — Was he? Hang on but – is he not dead?

   — I just told yeh. He was poisoned.

   — A good while – did he not die ages ago?

   — 2004.

   — So, why – just to be clear. He was the Palestinian fella, yeah?

   — Yeah.

   — With the scarf.

   — That's Yasser.

   — So, why did it take so long to find this ou'? Was it the HSE did the tests?

   — They had to dig him up – exhume him, like – to prove it.

   — Wha' was it – Chinese?

   — Why would the fuckin' Chinese poison Yasser Arafat? No, the smart money's on the Israelis.

   — No – the food, I meant.

   — Chinese food?

   — Yeah.

   — For fuck sake.

   — Are yeh seriously tellin' me there isn't a Chinese takeaway in Bethlehem?

   — Listen—

   — Kung Po Camel.

   — It was radioactive polonium.

   — Then it was the Russians. That's their department. Or—

   — Wha'?

   — The Shinners.

   — Sinn Féin killed Yasser Arafat?

   — Maybe.

— Come on – fuckin' how?

— Shergar.

— The horse?

— They sold him to the Chinese.

— The Palestinian Chinese?

— An' the Russians injected the stuff into Shergar. The Kung Po camel was really Kung Po poisoned racehorse.

— What abou' the Israelis?

— They hadn't a clue.

7-11-13

— Was Gerry Adams in the IRA?

— Is he dead?

— No. Was he in the RA?

— 'Course he was.

— He keeps sayin' he wasn't.

— He's lyin'.

— How d'yeh know?

— It's obvious.

— But how can yeh know? For certain, like. Were you in the IRA?

— Don't be fuckin' thick. Yeh might as well ask me did I play for Tranmere Rovers.

— Now you're the one bein' fuckin' thick. Tranmere Rovers never shot an' 'disappeared' innocent people. Did they?

— Not as far as we know. But, look it, John Aldridge managed them for a while an' Aldo would never do annythin' like tha'. Or anny of the Italia 90 squad.

— What about Roy?

— Roy wasn't in Italy.

— But Adams.

— He's lyin'.

— Yeah. Why, but?

— He's been sayin' it for fuckin' years. It's part of the story – the fuckin' narrative.

— So he can't back down?

— He can. But he won't. But I'll tell yeh wha' he can do.

— Wha'?

— He can fuck off to his cottage in Donegal an' live with his memories.

— Retire?

— Yep. Get off the stage an' let Mary Lou an' the other young fella take over. It must kill all those relatives every time tha' lyin' prick opens his mouth.

5-12-13

— See Ireland is the best country in the world for business.

— Fuck that drivel.

— It's official – it was in a magazine.

— *Shoot*?

— *Forbes*.

— Yeh know wha' that fuckin' means then? Just change 'best country' to 'country where you can do what yeh want and no one'll give much of a fuck', then you'll know why we're top o' the list.

— Ah now, that's a bit cynical.

— 'Young, educated workforce' means 'no tax'.

— Okay, okay – sit down. Where are we on Nigella?

— We're not on Nigella. That's the problem. She's a great young one.

— She's fifty-three.

— Exactly.

— She took cocaine.

— Even better. I love her. Anyway, she only took the cocaine when her first husband was dyin'.

— So she says.

— Yeh doubt her? Yeh cunt. When my first wife died—

— Hang on, hang on – fuck. Wha' first wife? Were you married before?

— No.

— Then what the fuck are yeh on abou'?

— Empathy.

— Wha'?!

— I imagined I had a first wife, dyin', like – just to see if I'd snort cocaine as well.

— And did yeh?

— Ah, yeah.

— Wha' was she like?
— The first wife?
— Yeah.
— Lovely.
— A bit like Nigella – was she?
— A bit, yeah.
— Just like mine, so.

— See Mandela's after pushin' Nigella off the front pages.

— Anyone else, I'd've been furious.

— Great man.

— That's puttin' it fuckin' mildly. Just walkin' out of tha' jail – d'yeh remember?

— I never thought somethin' as ordinary as watchin' someone goin' for a walk could be so incredible.

— D'you remember the Dunne Stores women?

— The strikers? I do, yeah. The wife's cousin was one o' them.

— Amazin', really. There we were, eatin' South African oranges an' tha'—

— Outspan.

— That's right – Jesus. And your woman on the checkout—

— Was it Mary Manning?

— Think so. She refuses to handle them. An' she's suspended an' there's the strike an' we all stop buyin' the oranges an' then the government bans them.

— Tha' would've been before Mandela got out o' jail.

— Yeah. Great fuckin' women.

— Nigella would've joined them.

— Probably, yeah. And d'you remember the day he came to Dublin?

— Same day the Irish team came home from Italy.

— That's righ' – Italia 90.

— Best tribute to him really, isn't it? The best Irish footballer ever an' the best politician in the world, side by side in the one chant.

— OOH AHH PAUL McGRATH'S DA – SAY OOH AAH PAUL McGRATH'S DA.

— We're out of the Bailout an'anyway. A nation once again, wha'.

— Fuck the fuckin' Bailout.

— What's wrong with yeh? Are yeh not happy tha' you can have your pint without worryin' tha' Merkel will whip it away from yeh?

— I'll tell yeh what's wrong with me.

— Go on.

— Fuckin' *Lawrence of Arabia*.

— Wha'?

— I go home a few nights ago an' she's cryin' – in the kitchen.

— Merkel?

— Fuck off. The wife.

— Why?

— I told yeh – *Lawrence of Arabia*.

— Was he in the kitchen as well?

— Fuck off. She's not cryin' like when Whitney died. She's really bawlin'. Fuckin' inconsolable.

— Cos o' Lawrence?

— Peter O'Toole, yeah. Turns out, all these years, she's fuckin' loved him – adored him. From fuckin' afar.

— Ah, that's just—

— He was tall, yeah?

— Yeah.

— Am I?

— Yeh would be, if you were up on a camel.

— He had beautiful blue eyes.

— Fuckin' beautiful?

— Wha' colour are mine?

— Kind o' grey an' red.

— Not blue.

— Not really. Maybe she just thought he was a good actor. Hang on but—. Is this a Fernando Torres thing? Did you fancy him too?

- - -

— An' now you have to share him with the missis? Is that it?

- - -

28-12-13

— How was the Christmas?

— Code fuckin' Red.

— Wha' happened?

— The mother-in-law.

— I thought she died.

— The new one.

— Oh fuck.

— Annyway. They all come to the house – the whole gang, like. An' she reacts badly to the stuffin'. A Nigella recipe, as it happens. Sausage meat an' Red Bull.

— Sounds lovely.

— Yeah, but she started expandin'.

— Well, it was the Christmas dinner. We all fuckin' expand.

— Really quickly. Like a thing in a fillum.

— Fuck.

— Exactly wha' I said. Anyway, then there's the lotto – who'll bring her to A an' E. An' they're all lookin' at me. Cos, like – A. I'm the fuckin' host, an' B. I have the van an' your woman's gettin' even bigger, so we'll be just about able to get her in the side door. But—

— Wha'?

— Well, it's Christmas. I want to stay at home with me family.

— But—

— Anyway. I say – listen to this. I say – as a matter of principle, like – I'm not willin' to bring anyone to hospital until I'm assured tha' the car-parkin' charge isn't goin' to top up some chief executive's salary.

— Jesus.

— Well, it seemed clever when I was sayin' it.

31-12-13

— How was your year?

— Ah, fuck off.

— Same here.

— Same shite.

— Death an' fuckin' disaster.

— I was shavin' this mornin', righ', an' there was this huge fuckin' hair growin' out of me ear. Two inches long, it was.

— An' tha' was your year's work, was it?

— Overnight. It wasn't there when I was brushin' the teeth last nigh'.

— Jesus, are your teeth in your ear as well?

— Fuck off. It's growin' old. Every fuckin' day – a bit less. I can hardly remember the names of me kids. The grandkids are fuckin' impostors.

— But yeh know, the worst thing about this year is findin' out the Yanks are watchin' us.

— Not me an' you, like.

— Yeah.

— Why the fuck would they be watchin' us? Now, like – here?

— Maybe.

— I thought it was only emails an' twitters an' tha'. So, if we change the order from two pints, say, to two pink gins, they'll tell Obama?

— They might.

— We'd better stick to the pints, so. To be on the safe side.

— Yeah. Fuckin' worryin', though, isn't it? Happy New Year, by the way.

— Fuck sake – I'm not fuckin' deaf!

— I wasn't talkin' to you. I was talkin' to Obama.

— See the Everly Brother died.

— Saw tha'. Sad.

— The lungs.

— Fuckin' cruel, isn't it? He gave so much pleasure to people usin' them lungs, for decades, like – more than fifty years. An' then they go an' fuckin' kill him.

— That's life.

— You said it, bud.

— 'Cathy's Clown'.

— Great song.

— Before our time, but, weren't they – a bit?

— No. No, I know what yeh mean. I don't remember seein' them on *Tops o' the Pops* or annythin'. But when you heard them on the radio—

— You always knew it was the Everlys.

— Exactly.

— An' it was always brilliant.

— Exactly – yeah.

—'Bye Bye Love'.

— There now – here's somethin'. My mother sang that every mornin' when me da was goin' to work. Goin' out the back door, like.

— Ah, that's nice. Isn't it?

— Yeah.

— That's a great memory to have. Cos o' Phil Everly.

— She sang it at the funeral as well.

— In the church?

— At the grave.

— God. Tha' must've been somethin'.

— It was. We all joined in at the end. '*Bye bye, my love, goodbye.*'

— They loved each other.
— They did.
— So, how come you're such a miserable cunt?
— Well, I can't blame Phil.

— Yeh know the way we're goin' to be payin' for the water?

— Well, fair enough. It hasn't rained since this mornin'.

— And yeh know the way this new company, Irish Water—

— Good name.

— At least it's in English.

— They prob'ly paid a gang o' fuckin' consultants to find the best way to get across the point that they're Irish an' they'll be sellin' the water.

— That's the thing, but. They've paid fifty million to consultants. But, like, what is a consultant?

— A cunt.

— That all?

— With a jockey's bollix.

— A cunt with a jockey's bollix?

— Basically. A fuckin' chancer who's happy enough to take money from a useless bunch o' pricks who haven't the guts or the brains to make their own decisions, an' call it expertise.

— But, say—

— An' they all went to the same schools. The pricks an' the cunts. It's business as usual in Ireland fuckin' Inc.

— But—

— An' it's our money.

— Will we have another pint?

— I've the money for the round but I don't have the consultancy fee.

— Wha' fuckin' consultancy fee?

— D'yeh expect me to answer tha' question on me own? 'Will we have another pint?' It could take fuckin' years.

31-1-14

— See all the Uggs tha' got stolen?

    — Wha' – the whole family? The kids as well?

    — What are you on abou'?

    — The Uggs, tha' live over the bookie's.

    — That's only their nickname.

    — Fuck – is it?

    — I meant the boots. That all the young ones wear.

    — And one or two o' the oul' ones.

    — Anyway, there was a million quids' worth stolen.

    — Where?

    — Cork.

    — Ah well.

    — The lads were caught but, like, some o' the Uggs got away – you with me?

    — Grand.

    — An', Cork bein' Cork, they've ended up in Dublin.

    — That's not a pair yeh have on yeh there, is it?

    — No – fuck off. These are desert boots.

    — They're nice.

    — I've had them a few years. Anyway. I know a chap might be able to find some – Uggs, like. Especially suitable for girls with different-sized feet.

    — Ah, for fuck—

    — No – it's a scientifically proven fact. We all have different-sized feet but it's usually not tha' big of a difference. But anyway, these Uggs would be a fuckin' godsend for a young one with, say, one size-four foot an' the other one size seven.

    — Which is which?

    — Left, four. Right, seven.

    — I'll get workin' on it.

11-2-14

— See Shirley Temple died.

— There's a thing.

— Wha'?

— Shirley Temple. There was a fella in my class – in primary school. He'd curly hair – loads of it, like. An' a baby face. Mind you, we all had baby faces. We were only fuckin' six or somethin'. But the teacher – a righ' fuckin' monster – I can't remember her name. But anyway, she called him Shirley Temple. An' it stuck.

— The poor cunt.

— All his life.

— Did he die?

— Today.

— No. Same as Shirley?

— Same day, not sure abou' the time. Yeah, he was always called Shirley. An' he went bald in his thirties.

— Hang on. Tha' Shirley? Is she a man?

— Different one – you're barkin' up the wrong Shirley. Tha' Shirley just shaves her head – it's a lifestyle choice, like. You wouldn't've known this lad. He moved to England, somewhere.

— To get away from bein' called Shirley.

— Tha' an' a job, yeah.

— Come here, but. Shirley Temple. The real one, like – the original one. You know – all those fillums. The little dresses an' 'On the Good Ship Lollipop' an' tha'.

— Wha'?

— It was fuckin' weird. Wasn't it?

— Very fuckin' weird.

7-3-14

— See the city's full o' Nazis.

— Wha'?

— Nazis.

— In Dublin?

— So I heard. Bono was talkin' to them.

— Well, tha' would turn anyone into a Nazi, havin' to listen to tha' cunt. Wha' was Bono doin' talkin' to fuckin' Nazis?

— There's a conference of them. In the Convention Centre. The Nazis an' Fine Gael.

— Hold on. Fine Gael aren't fuckin' Nazis.

— Merkel's there as well.

— She's not a fuckin' Nazi. She's only a German. Yeh can't be callin' the Germans Nazis. They're grand, the Germans. I like Merkel.

— I kind o' do as well. There's somethin' about her – she doesn't give a shite.

— That's it. She's one o' the lads. Annyway, look it. It's the European People's Party that's in the Convention Centre. They're not Nazis. They just look a bit odd.

— No uniforms, no?

— No.

— Shite. I was goin' to bring the grandkids down to have a look at them.

— No, they're just right of centre. A bunch of heartless cunts, but not Nazis – in fairness. Borin' as fuck, I'd say. Imagine goin' for a pint with a gang of Fine Gaelers an' Christian Democrats from Belgium.

— An' Bono.

— Fuck sake. Give me the Nazis, anny day.

11-3-14

— See Christine Buckley died.

— Saw tha'. Sad.

— Very sad. Great woman.

— Great fuckin' woman.

— Wha' was the name o' tha' place, where she exposed the abuse?

— Goldenbridge.

— That's it. Hard to imagine a place with a name like tha' could be so fuckin' evil, isn't it?

— I know wha' yeh mean. You'd kind of expect hobbits in a place called Goldenbridge.

— Well, tha' was the problem, wasn't it? If the place had been run by hobbits, they'd have looked after those poor kids properly. A bit of love an' tha'. Not like the fuckin' nuns, batterin' them.

— It's nearly twenty years.

— Wha'?

— Since tha' programme Christine Buckley was in.

— Yeh serious?

— Yeah. 1996. Said it on the radio. Is the country any better, d'yeh think?

— Well, if it is, it's because o' Christine Buckley, an' them.

— I met her once.

— Did yeh?

— Corner o' Mary Street an' Jervis Street. She was standin' there, like she was waitin' for someone. An' I knew I knew her, but I didn't know her – d'yeh know wha' I mean? I knew her face. An' I said, 'Are you—?' An' she goes, 'That's right – Diana Ross.' An' she bursts ou' laughin'.

8-4-14

— Peaches Geldof.

— Jesus, man, it's sad.

— So fuckin' – just—. Sad.

— I know nothin' about her. Except she's Geldof's daughter an' she was in the magazines.

— She was only twenty-five.

— Terrifyin'. It'd have yeh wanderin' around the house, checkin' the windows.

— Textin' the kids an' grandkids, makin' sure they're alrigh'.

— Exactly. I drove past my young one's flat, just to make sure. I didn't go in or anythin'. I just wanted to – I don't know – be useful, or somethin'. A father – yeh know?

— Yeah. An' Mickey Rooney died as well.

— I know nothin' about him either.

— A child actor, by all accounts.

— Not fuckin' recently, but.

— He was in a lot o' fillums with Judy Garland. So they said on the radio.

— The only one o' hers I seen is *The Wizard of Oz*, an' he's not in tha', I don't think. Unless he was one o' the hobbits.

— Munchkins.

— Yeah. Or – now that I think of it – was he the friendly lion?

— The cowardly lion.

— Fuck off now. There was nothin' stoppin' him from bein' both friendly an' cowardly. It's easily managed.

— It wasn't him. Tha' was Bert Lahr.

— Okay.

— She had two kids.

— Saw tha'. Two little lads.

- - - - - -

- - - - - - - - - - -

22-4-14

— See David Moyes is gone.

— The wrong man at the wrong time.

— That's not wha' you were sayin' last year.

— No, I always had me doubts – in fairness. I never doubted his honesty or his work ethic—

— 'He'll be perfect for the job, wait an' see.'

— Are you fuckin' readin' tha'?

— 'He's mini-Fergie. A cranky cunt – and I mean that as a compliment.'

— A little black book? Where'd tha' come from?

— 'He's an excellent man motivator and his tactical acumen has long been under-fuckin'-estimated.'

— Yeh fuckin' prick.

— 'He'll be in the job for twenty years. That's the United way. We're not like other clubs.'

— Okay. Did yeh never hear of fuckin' irony, no?

— Goin' back a few pages. 'Whoever replaces Fergie, he'll be given the time to establish himself. We're not called Man Unitedski.'

— Yeh cunt.

— Here's another one. 'That's why we're the biggest club in the world. We have values.'

— Well, come here, yeh cunt. You're not the only one with a black book. Here's one from way back. 'There's no way I'd ever marry tha' one. She has a mouth on her like a fuckin' can opener.'

— I never said fuckin' tha'.

— 22nd of April, 1981.

— Well, the journalists got it right, annyway.

— About David Moyes?

— Yeah.

— They're fuckin' brilliant, aren't they?

— He was never the right man for the job.

— Never.

— We couldn't see it at first but – thank fuck now – the journalists could.

— He wasn't even the righ' man at Everton.

— He was shite there too.

— For eleven years. Pulled the fuckin' wool over everyone's eyes.

— It took Roberto Martinez to rescue them. To move them up from sixth to fuckin' fifth.

— A genius, tha' fella.

— Buyin' Aiden McGeady.

— Stroke o' genius, tha'.

— From Red Star Glasgow, or wherever the fuck he found him.

— Changed the course o' the club's history.

— World history.

— Meanwhile Moyes bought Juan Mata.

— A shite player.

— A shite player who was one of the world's most exciting players, ignored—

— Inex-fuckin'-plicably.

— By José Mourinho.

— Until Moyes bought him an' he became shite overnight.

— Cos o' Moyes.

— Arrives in Manchester in a helicopter an' immediately turns to shite.

— An' we never knew.
— But the journalists did.
— Cunts.
— What about Ryan Giggs?
— He's only temporary.
— Yeah, but—
— Wha'?
— Is the physio's wife safe, d'yeh think?
— I'd have me doubts.

25-4-14

— See using your phone while drivin's been made illegal.

— It's been illegal for years.

— Yeah, but it's really illegal now. A thousand-quid fine if you're caught.

— Yeah, but it's only for a few days. It'll be back to normal after the weekend.

— Shockin' though, isn't it? First the drink.

— Then the smokin'.

— Now yeh can't even drive up the quays an' do your online shoppin' at the same time.

— There's no pleasure left in life, is there?

— Last week – listen. I hit a woman with a pram – outside Artaine Castle, righ'. When I was havin' a quick gawk at the Paddy Power's website. But – and this is my point, this is why it's bad law. If I hadn't been choosin' a horse, I'd have been goin' way quicker and I'd have killed the poor woman. And, in fairness, she saw my point, once we got her down off the roof.

— What about the baby?

— Wha' baby?

— In the fuckin' pram.

— There wasn't a baby. It was her husband – her fuckin' life partner. She was bringin' him home from the Goblet.

— Was he hurt?

— Fuck'm. He was textin'. So he wasn't in control of his vehicle.

30-4-14

— See Bob Hoskins is after dyin'.

— Sad, tha'.

— Hadn't seen him in anythin' for a while.

— He mustn't have been well.

— No.

— He was one o' the lads, wasn't he?

— Brilliant. Just his face – the expressions, yeh know.

— Fabulous. From the very beginnin'. Fuckin' way back.

— *Pennies from Heaven*. D'you remember tha' one?

— I do, yeah. Brilliant. Your one, Gemma Craven, was in it as well.

— I used to like her.

— She was Irish, wasn't she?

— We won't hold that against her.

— *Mona Lisa.*

— There was no way *she* was fuckin' Irish.

— The fillum.

— Yeah, yeah – brilliant.

— I didn't like *Roger Rabbit.*

— Know wha' yeh mean. He was an irritatin' cunt. But Hoskins was good.

— Can't think of a bad one he was in.

— Cos he was in them.

— Probably, yeah – good point.

— The best, but. *The Long Good Friday.*

— Ah, Jesus. Magnificent.

— D'you remember the end, in the car, when he knows he's fucked?

— His face – yeah. Brilliant.

— He was frightened, grand, but he looked nearly happy as well. Impressed, like, tha' they'd snared him.

— D'yeh think he looked like tha' this time?
— When he knew he was dyin'?
— Yeah.
— I hope so.
— Me too.

3-5-14

— See Gerry Adams is after bein' arrested.

 — No, you're wrong there. He went voluntarily.

 — But—

 — An' while we're at it, he was never a member o' the IRA.

 — That's a load o'—

 — And, in fact, he was never even called Gerry Adams.

 — Wha'—?!

 — An' there's no such thing as the IR fuckin' A.

 — Hang on now—

 — There never was a man called Gerry Adams. It's all a creation of the London and Dublin administrations, in cahoots with the media, to undermine Sinn Féin's election campaign.

 — You've fuckin' lost me, bud.

 — If there is such a place as Dublin – an' I have me doubts there as well.

 — You're on your own.

 — Not for the first fuckin' time.

 — Gerry Adams isn't Gerry Adams. That's the theory, yeah?

 — Stands to fuckin' reason. It's the only logical conclusion. He's all a myth. The beard an' the teeth. An' the trigger finger. Did I say tha'? I hope not. I fuckin' deny it.

 — They've made him up?

 — I think so, yeah. The only alternative is tha' he made himself up an' got a bit carried away.

 — What abou' Mary Lou?

 — What abou' her?

 — Is she real?

 — Big time.

4-5-14

— 'What A Wonderful World'.

— Fuck off.

— Louis Armstrong.

— Fuck off.

— Great song.

— Fuck off.

— Number one in May 1968.

— Fuck off.

— The last time Sunderland beat Man United at Old Trafford.

— Fuck off.

— It stayed at number one for four weeks.

— Fuck off.

— Ah now. Georgie Best scored for United.

— Fuck off.

— Good oul' Giggsy.

— Fuck off.

— An' the Class o' '92.

— Fuck off.

— Playin' the United way.

— Fuck off or I'm leavin'.

- - - - -

- - - - -

- - - - -

- - - - -

- - - - - - - -

- -

— Biggest-sellin' single of 1968.

— Fuck off.

9-6-14

— See Rik Mayall died.

— Sad.

— Desperate. Younger than us.

— Remember *The Young Ones*?

— Ah, for fuck sake. There was nothin' like it.

— 'His name's Rick. The P is silent.' Best line, ever.

— I always associate *The Young Ones* with me first video.

— Yeah – yeah. They both came at about the same time, didn't they?

— I'd tape *The Young Ones* an' watch it when I got home. There was once – when I got the video, like. A chap in work gave me a dodgy one. *Debbie Does—*

— Dallas.

— No – *Dungarvan*. It was Irish-made – made me proud. It was fuckin' rough, I'll tell yeh. But, annyway. I came in an' my ma was in the kitchen. She was stayin' a few days.

— She only lived around the corner.

— Yeah, but me da was howlin' at the moon.

— Grand.

— So, she says, 'You said you'd tape *Coronation Street* for me.' An' I thought, 'Oh, bollix – she's after seein' *Debbie*.

— Oh Jaysis—

— No, it was grand. I'd taped *The Young Ones* over *Corrie*. I made her watch it with me, an' the kids all got up to see, cos she was laughin' so much.

— That's nice.

— It is, isn't it?

11-6-14

— The mother and baby homes.

— Shockin'.

— That's the thing, but.

— Wha'?

— Yeh kind o' get used to it, don't yeh. The stories – all the fuckin' misery. It's been goin' on for years. Am I makin' sense?

— Kind of. I think so, yeah.

— I thought it was over, d'yeh know what I mean? All the inquiries, and the bishops an' tha'.

— Consigned to history, like.

— Exactly – spot on. An' then, when they're on about eight hundred babies dumped in a septic tank, or whatever the fuck—

— Nuns with buckets o' babies.

— Yeah – I mean, I haven't seen a nun in fuckin' years, with or without a bucket. They're like the fuckin' dinosaurs.

— Long gone.

— We'll only be seein' them in cartoons soon. But then— Yesterday, I'm readin' abou' the kids in the mother an' baby homes tha' were used for vaccine tests. In 1973. An' I think, 'Oh – my – Jaysis.'

— I was workin' in 1973.

— Me too. Or, I wanted to be. But those kids, like.

— They're younger than us.

— Much younger than us.

— So, it's not history, is it?

— No, it fuckin' isn't. It's current affairs.

112

23-6-14

— Three pints.

— One'll do me.

— No. Three pints is a binge.

— Says who?

— Heard it on the radio. Some fuckin' survey, or somethin'.

— That's fuckin' mad. I'd need three pints before I decide whether to go on a fuckin' binge or not.

— I worked it out earlier. I've been on a fuckin' binge since 1975. Three pints, two or three times a month, constitutes harmful drinkin'.

— So – wha'? You've been drinkin' yourself to death for nearly forty years?

— Apparently.

— Well, you're not very fuckin' good at it, are yeh? Yeh look grand.

— Thanks. I'll tell yeh wha' the problem is. An' it's not the drinkin'.

— Wha'?

— The drinkin's grand. I did me own survey an' most Irish people are happy enough with the amount they drink.

— How many did yeh talk to?

— Just the one.

— Fair enough.

— The problem is, the fuckers – the doctors – tha' do these surveys. They haven't a fuckin' clue what a good binge is. They've no righ' to use the word.

— It's ours.

— Exactly. So they can fuck off. Three pints in a row isn't a national crisis. It's a fuckin' necessity. It's probably the only thing tha' stops us from bein' Swiss.

113

25-6-14

— Yeh have to admire Suarez, all the same.

  — Go on – why?

  — Well, if yeh were goin' to bite an Italian—

  — Sophia Loren.

— She wasn't playin' last night, I don't think. I didn't see her on the pitch.

  — She was on the bench.

  — Grand. You're Suarez.

  — Okay.

— You feel the irresistible fuckin' urge to bite an opponent.

  — Okay.

  — You go down through the Italian team sheet.

  — Like a menu.

  — Exactly.

  — Pirlo an' chips.

— There now – good man. You've put your fuckin' finger on it. You wouldn't go for Chiellini an' chips, sure yeh wouldn't?

  — Too skinny.

— Too fuckin' hard. He'd knock the livin' fuck out of yeh. Pirlo wouldn't even notice if yeh bit him. He's too laid back.

  — An' hairy.

— Movin' on. He – Suarez, like – he was the same when he was decidin' which o' the Chelsea squad he was goin' to sample. He didn't go for one o' the little lads. Oscar or Hazard. He bit a fuckin' Serb.

  — A fuckin' warlord.

— I'm tellin' yeh. Suarez should have his own programme – on the telly, like.

  — *Eat With Luis.*

— A football celebrity cannibalism quiz.
— With Robbie Savage.
— An' the other cunt.
— Jamie Redknapp.
— He'll do.